SMART MOVES

A KID'S GUIDE TO SELF-DEFENSE

CHRISTOPHER J. GOEDECKE
ROSMARIE HAUSHERR

ACKNOWLEDGMENTS We would like to thank all of the children and adults who participated in the production of this book, particularly the twelve children who were photographed for the main chapters: Patricia Andrade, Ignacio Borderes, Daniel Chen, Erin Dupack, Tommy Ellis, Deanna Ford, Robert Hopkins, Aja Houston, Ivan Martinez, Justin Sobers, Frederick (Fritz) Staudmayer, and Joshua Weisenbeck. We are grateful to the Chatham Club and the Madison YMCA for the use of their facilities. We are also thankful to Swiss photographer Felix Wey for his phototechnical assistance and professional skill. The publisher would like to thank Dr. Evan Baltazzi for sharing his insightful reading of the material in this book.

PHOTOGRAPH AND ILLUSTRATION ACKNOWLEDGMENTS The following have generously granted permission to reprint their work: page 32 (medieval warriors), courtesy of Bildarchiv der Zentralbibliothek, Luzern; page 59 (football players), courtesy of Clarion Books/Houghton Mifflin Company, from *Whose Hat Is That?* by Ron Roy, photo by Rosmarie Hausherr; pages 11 (bird), 18 (tiger), 25, 33, and 38 (boxers), and 39 (martial arts master and movie stars), courtesy of Keystone Press, Zurich; page 30 (acupuncture diagram), courtesy of Weatherhill, Inc., from *The Layman's Guide to Acupuncture* by Yoshio Manaka and Ian A. Urquhart; page 40 (karate master), courtesy of Paul Vigilante; and page 48 (samurai warriors), courtesy of Weatherhill, Inc., from *Classical Bujutsu* by Donn F. Draeger. The *chikara* pictograph found throughout this book was created by Shiman Eido Roshi, Abbot of the Zen Studies Society, a parent organization of Dai Bosatsu Zendo Kondi-Ji.

SIMON & SCHUSTER BOOKS FOR YOUNG READERS
An imprint of Simon & Schuster Children's Publishing Division
1230 Avenue of the Americas
New York, New York 10020
Text copyright © 1995 by Christopher J. Goedecke
Photographs copyright © 1995 by Rosmarie Hausherr
Illustrations and arrows on pages 41–44 copyright © 1995 by John Stephens
All rights reserved including the right of reproduction in whole or in part in any form.
SIMON & SCHUSTER BOOKS FOR YOUNG READERS is a trademark of Simon & Schuster.
Book design by Christy Hale
Manufactured in the United States of America
10 9 8 7 6 5 4 3 2 1

Library of Congress Cataloging-in-Publication Data
Goedecke, Christopher J.
Smart Moves : a kid's guide to self-defense / by Christopher J.
Goedecke ; photographs by Rosmarie Hausherr.
        p.   cm.
Includes bibliographical references and index.
ISBN 0-689-80294-3
1. Self-defense for children—Juvenile literature. 2. Self-defense for children—Psychological aspects—Juvenile literature. 3. Bullying—Juvenile literature. 4. Assault and battery—Prevention—Juvenile literature. [1. Self-defense. 2. Bullies.] I. Hausherr, Rosmarie, ill. II. Title.
GV1111.4.G64   1995   613.6'6—dc20   94-36863

The *chikara* used throughout this book is a Japanese pictograph that represents a person holding up a mountain. It symbolizes energy or force.

One Bridge to Safety

During the past decade, I have queried thousands of children in my classes and in their schools about their knowledge of self-protection. They reveal a startling lack of knowledge and skills about avoiding physical conflicts and minimizing pain or injury when such incidents are unavoidable. Even well-intentioned parents often pass along to their children conflicting, impractical, or scant advice.

Though healthy young people never willingly call personal danger upon themselves, unprovoked physical aggressions happen all the time. Whether it is a bully's shove or a stranger's violent assault, these incidents demand immediate self-protective responses.

A great deal of knowledge exists today to help children cope with physical conflicts. Psychologists understand much about the roots of aggressive behavior and its emotional impact on victims. The popularity of martial arts among young people attests to their hunger for control in hostile environments. Through martial arts and self-defense programs, child protection awareness courses, and even contact sports, many young people have acquired personal techniques and strategies to enhance their safety and to develop their self-control and self-esteem.

This book builds one bridge to safety by outlining commonsense techniques, ideas, and behaviors for dealing with aggressive or violent physical encounters. The guidelines offered in this book are served best by sharing your ideas, feelings, personal histories, and protective traditions with your children. Proper self-defense awareness and training can prepare young people to meet physical dangers with a healthy moral perspective, backed by intelligent and responsible actions.

It is given that many self-defense activities involving two people can result in some type of injury to one or both participants. Without the personal supervision of a trained professional to guide a child through the movements of any particular technique, details may be overlooked. Regretfully, it is impossible to convey the many subtleties of self-defense within the scope of this book, nor can any book portray universal technique for all situations. What this book does offer, however, are many new ideas and choices, and the opportunity for kids to understand that they hold powers they only had dreamed they could possess.

Contents

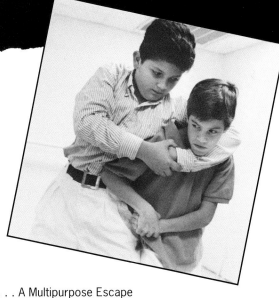

Part 3   A PLAN FOR VICTORY

Part 4   WHAT IF IT HAPPENED TO YOU?

Part 1

UNDERSTANDING SELF-DEFENSE

Imagine over five billion people living under one roof. The happy and the hateful, the healing and the harmful, the clear-minded and the confused are all mixed together. Problems are bound to occur. This describes our planet today.

Because the world spins both safe and threatening webs, anyone can suddenly become a victim. To confront a harmful person without protective powers is dangerous and inadvisable. For this reason, self-defense powers were developed. In most cultures, these skills are handed down, from family elders to their young, or from teacher to student, warrior to apprentice, master to disciple. They give people the ability to fight for their rights and their lives.

"Would you like the power to protect yourself?" the tall speaker asks a group of students. He is a self-defense expert and karate master. Many of his students simply call him *Sensei* (teacher). Twelve eager children raise their hands.

"It is time to pass this special power over to you. Let's start by discussing Ted's problem."

Would you like the power to protect yourself?

TED'S PROBLEM—A TRUE STORY

Ted walked across the school yard. Someone shouted, "Hey! Teddy bear!" Unfamiliar voices laughed. Ted turned around and saw several boys teasing and taunting him. One boy strode up to Ted and shoved him backward. Ted fell onto the hard ground. As he tried to get up, the boy kicked him in the ribs. The blow was painful. He lost his breath and became afraid. Surprise and shock flashed across his face. Anger welled in his throat.

Ted was torn between crying and blurting out, "Why are you hurting me?" He did not know whether to run or stand up and fight. The bully laughed and threatened to kick him again. Ted's mind raced to find a solution to his problem.

WHAT SHOULD TED DO?

Do you think Ted should fight? Could he defeat the larger boy, or ward off the gang? What if Ted loses his temper and seriously hurts one of the bullies, even by accident? What if Ted gets injured retaliating in self-defense?

Do you think Ted should run? Will he be fast enough to escape? How will he feel if his schoolmates call him a "chicken" for running away? What if Ted thinks of himself as a coward? Does Ted have any other choices of action besides fighting or running?

Of course, Ted never thought he would be picked on.

WHAT IF _YOU_ HAD TO DEFEND YOURSELF?

How would you react if someone threatened and then started to hurt you? Would you be unsure whether to yell, cry, fight, or run? Could you defend yourself intelligently?

Of course, Ted never thought _he_ would be picked on. Yet peaceful people become victims every day, all over the world. Children, teens, even adults get bullied, pushed around, punched, slapped, mocked, scared, beaten up, robbed, molested, abducted, or raped. Has anyone ever made fun of you, pushed you around, punched you, or touched you when you did not want them to? This is called abuse. No matter what form abuse takes, it is never right.

Nobody likes to be a victim. After Ted's incident, he decided he never wanted to be embarrassed, harassed, scared, or kicked again. A friend told him that if he knew self-defense, he would be better prepared for facing any bully. So he joined a neighborhood martial arts school. Like thousands of young boys and girls throughout the world, Ted began to study ways to protect himself from physical conflict.

What Is Self-Defense?

"What did he learn?" curiosity prompts Deanna to ask.

"Ted learned that self-defense is not about fighting back. It's about fighting smart!" Sensei explains. "Anyone can throw punches and kicks without specific training. But self-defense is not an 'eye-for-an-eye' attitude like getting even, or getting revenge. It's about *not getting injured.* The best self-defense considers your safety first and tries to find a peaceful solution to a problem.

"In any violent situation, no matter who you are or what you know, you can always get hurt. Self-defense skills never make anyone invincible," Sensei continues. "Even the greatest boxers in the world take hard punches during bouts. But some young people forget that invincibility is only for superheroes in the movies and on TV. A young karate student asked his teacher one day how to shoot a *fireball*! These powers are not real."

Self-defense is simply a tool. It teaches you how to think smart and act safely to reduce fear, pain, or injury.

Self-defense is not about fighting back. It's about fighting smart!

REMEMBER

> **Self-defense is a *natural right*.** All human beings have a natural right to protect themselves from injury by others.

> **Self-defense is a *survival instinct*.** An instinct is a powerful impulse or drive, like the feeling of hunger. We are born to live and will do anything to stay alive. This strong instinct is also evident in animals. They will defend themselves to the death and valiantly protect their young from predators.

> **Self-defense is a *law*.** The law states that you have the right to use *reasonable force* to prevent injury to yourself. This law protects you from punishment if you must take appropriate action to stop another person from hurting you.

> **Self-defense is an *action*** in which our bodies and minds act together in a whole-person response.

Rights vs. Abilities

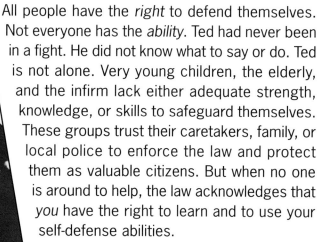

All people have the *right* to defend themselves. Not everyone has the *ability*. Ted had never been in a fight. He did not know what to say or do. Ted is not alone. Very young children, the elderly, and the infirm lack either adequate strength, knowledge, or skills to safeguard themselves. These groups trust their caretakers, family, or local police to enforce the law and protect them as valuable citizens. But when no one is around to help, the law acknowledges that *you* have the right to learn and to use your self-defense abilities.

Ted's bullies were offensive but he took no action to defend himself. Ted was unsure of his rights and his abilities.

An **OFFENSIVE** person is one who seeks to hurt another without a just cause and without any feelings for the other person's well-being.

A **DEFENSIVE** person is one who chooses, by taking protective action, not to be the victim.

Physical Actions vs. Feelings

Ramon *pushes* Richard for calling him a name. Jack *punches* Tony because he is angry. Mary *kicks* her friend Sue because she can't get her way. Brandon *verbally threatens* to beat up Raj after school. A bully *shoves* and then *kicks* Ted. Pushes, punches, grabs, slaps, kicks, and verbal threats are all types of physical actions. Physical actions are the front line of a problem.

Peter *fears* that Jack is going to start a fight with him. Peter *feels* nervous. He becomes quiet and still. He *feels* his heart racing and his mouth getting dry. Tommy *feels* weird after Bert hits him in the ear with a snowball. He *feels* like knocking Bert down even though Bert is his friend.

Under your skin, powerful sensations are aroused when you are threatened. These strong sensations are called emotions. Fear, anger, joy, sorrow, love, and hate are all emotions you can feel in your body, and they affect how you react to your problems. Peter felt so afraid that he could not move. Tommy felt so angry that he feared he would not control himself from lashing out at his friend.

Like many young people, Ted was confused about what action to take when his scary feelings erupted. He did not know how to use his feelings and physical actions as powerful survival tools. All of that was about to change for him.

Under your skin, powerful sensations are aroused when you are threatened.

Part 2 MASTERING YOUR SURVIVAL SKILLS

ou are now ready to master your powerful survival tools—new ideas, behaviors, and techniques that will give you *choices* and *control* when trouble unfolds and no one is around to help.

"I'm ready to learn!" Daniel eagerly announces.

"There are seven essential powers," Sensei responds.

POWER 1

Shape Ideas into Positive Action

Suppose you believe all dogs are friendly creatures. Your actions toward dogs will be kind. But if you believe dogs are vicious, your actions toward dogs will be cautious, fearful, and defensive. You will keep your distance. Suppose you have the cruel idea that dogs should be beaten. Then your actions will be mean and violent. You will tease, hit, or throw things at the dogs you come across.

Your ideas about dogs or people will shape your actions toward them. When you play with, run from, or kick a dog or a bully, you are acting out your beliefs. When you turn your ideas into action, it is called *behavior*.

Many of our ideas about solving conflicts are passed to us from others: our parents, relatives, teachers, friends, etc. Sometimes those ideas can be passed from generation to generation and handed down to you, whether you want them or not.

"If the other person starts it, you can finish it!" is common advice some fathers give their sons.

"My dad tells me to stand up to the bullies in my school," one of the group admits. "I don't want to fight. But my dad will think I'm a chicken."

"Well, I like fighting because I always win," another boy remarks.

"I'm sure the boy you beat up doesn't like it," the teacher responds. "One day he may gang up on you to get even. Then you'll have a war on your hands. Wars are terrible, even small ones. People always get hurt. Are you sure you aren't trying to impress your dad, an older brother, or your friends?

"It's never too late to change your ideas. Besides, some of them may have been handed down to you like secondhand clothes that don't fit anymore. Beliefs are changeable. Perhaps it's time to get rid of the bad ones. You don't have to share a negative idea just because someone else does," Sensei tells them.

"Changing an idea is less painful than mending a broken nose from a fight," Josh states. Everyone agrees.

If the idea of fighting back or running away makes you feel bad, find another action to make you feel good and that will lead to everyone's safety. For example, if you don't like hiding your feelings, then express them. It's okay to say, "Let's talk instead of fight." It's okay to avoid pain, injury, and insult. It's okay to ask for help when you're in trouble!

What are your ideas
about fighting or
protecting yourself?

Ivan: *"Fights make things worse. If you're in one, get it over with quickly."*

Robert: *"Fighting is stupid! People get hurt."*

Josh: *"If you have to defend yourself, be confident but not mean."*

Fritz: *"You should fight only as a last resort."*

Erin: *"Talk your way out of trouble, and block if they try to hit you."*

Aja: *"Bullies want attention. One way they get it is by fighting. I would be willing to trust a bully if she or he was willing to change."*

Not everyone agrees. That's okay. These are new ideas for many of the students.

SHARE AND COMPARE

At home Erin asks her family what they would do if someone tried to hurt them. Her eighty-four-year-old grandfather gives his granddaughter some advice. "Don't pick a fight unless you can win," he tells her. This is her dad's advice also. But Erin says that if she gets married and has children, she's going to tell them, "Don't start fights, even if you can win!" Erin doesn't believe in fighting at all.

Josh discovers that his dad got into a big fight while in military boot camp. He sent another cadet, who had attacked him with a broomstick, to the hospital. He felt awful that he had injured the cadet. He told Josh, "It's a terrible feeling to know that you hurt someone. Avoid fights whenever you can."

Aja lives with her divorced mom. Her mother tells her that when she was a young girl she was bullied for two years. She was miserable and did not know what to do. She is glad Aja is learning self-defense. She doesn't ever want Aja to be bullied.

"You all have so many different ideas," Sensei observes. "Maybe some positive seeds have been planted in your heads by sharing them with one another. Only positive thoughts lead to peace."

POWER **2** •
Face Your Feelings

What does your face reveal? Is it threatening or calming? A person's face can offer clues to one's feelings and possible actions. Clearly recognizing a face's message may help you to see or to avert trouble coming.

"It's time to face your feelings," Sensei declares. He hands out paper and colored markers. Everyone begins drawing angry, loving, mean, fearful, and happy faces on the paper.

If you want to face *your* feelings, get some paper and colored markers and draw what you would look like if you were threatened by a bully, if a strange adult tried to hurt you, if you hated someone, if someone made you fighting mad, if a monster scared you, if you were around your best friends and it was your birthday, and if you felt peace and love for the world.

Inner Firefights: Dealing with Feeling

Fear and anger are the most common feelings people have when they are threatened. When anger turns into rage or fear changes into terror or panic, you can lose control of your actions. That's how injuries occur. To avoid such a problem, you can learn to use the power of your fiery feelings constructively rather than let them burn out of control.

Fight, Flee, or Freeze?

A stranger lunges from behind a bush at a young boy. The boy is startled and frightened. His legs begin to shake. His heart pops into his throat. Weird sensations churn inside him. His legs feel like stone. The boy doesn't fight or run. He is momentarily frozen in fear, unable to fight or flee. His trigger of action is jammed.

There is a powerful, primitive mechanism in animals and humans called the "fight or flight" reaction, set off by the first signs of danger: Your body becomes supercharged with energy. You need to fight with every ounce of your strength or to escape from harm. But there is also another reaction to danger: You might freeze in panic or shock and become completely helpless.

Wild animals face many daily dangers. When threatened, they run or fight. They rarely freeze except to camouflage themselves. However, most humans aren't threatened every day, so we are not prepared for a powerful explosion of feelings. That is why overpowering feelings sometimes rivet some people helplessly to the ground.

What does fear feel like to you?

"My mouth gets dry."
"My legs feel shaky."
"I feel like throwing up."
"I want to run and hide."
"I get a headache."
"I start shaking."
"My legs get weak."
"My palms get sweaty."
"I feel like jelly."
"I get chills."
"My heart pounds."
"My body tingles."
"I feel butterflies in my stomach."
"I feel like I have a marble stuck in my throat."

"You have all described how your bodies alert and prepare you for survival action," Sensei explains. "Experiencing fear does not make you cowardly. It is your body's warning signal that trouble is near."

Experiencing fear does not make you cowardly. It is your body's warning signal that trouble is near.

Anger is the energy that gives you the raw power to deal with danger. Anger causes extra blood to be pumped into your limbs for action! That is why most angry people have a sudden urge to do something physical. Anger can make a person feel red-hot with power, or hopping and fighting mad. Anger is a healthy energy if it helps you out of trouble. But if your anger causes trouble, it is an unhealthy, destructive power.

Extinguishing Fiery Feelings

Fear and anger are healthy, normal reactions when you are threatened. However, if your fear or anger gets out of hand, try these exercises to put you back in control of your actions.

1 I AM OKAY

Don't deny or turn your feelings off. Like the great karate masters, you can learn to tap into the abundant power reserve of your feelings to meet any challenge. If you are threatened, repeat the statements below to remind yourself of the important role your feelings play in your safety.

I am okay; my fear is normal. My body is warning me something is wrong.

I am okay; my anger is normal. My body is energizing me for protection.

2 IN WITH THE GOOD AIR, OUT WITH THE BAD

Deep breathing, called "belly breathing," can soothe fearful or angry emotions. Simply take in a slow, deep breath through your nose. Let your belly fill and expand. Hold the air for a second, then slowly exhale. Inhaling and exhaling deeply, slowly, and rhythmically calms the nerves and relaxes the muscles.

3 THE TKO TEN COUNT

Give your excessive emotions a TKO (technical knockout) ten count. Whenever you feel a surge of fear or anger, it's because adrenaline, a muscle energizer, is pumping into your system. To work off the excess adrenaline, slowly count to ten while belly breathing. Counting anchors your mind to an easy task and will help you to remain clearheaded.

4 THE "EXPRESS" TRAIN

Strong feelings can often be reduced simply by expressing yourself and talking them out. It's okay to tell others what you're feeling. For example, you could say, "I am afraid (or angry) and I don't like it, but that is how I feel." It's healthier to give your strong feelings an "express train" out of your body.

5 THE HIGH ROAD ABOVE ANGER

Breaking things, having negative thoughts, or picking on other people is an unhealthy way to release your anger. This is the low road, the path of destruction where something or someone gets broken or hurt. People who behave this way have a problem. Rise above any destructive feelings by letting your anger out in peaceful, nonviolent ways. The furious boy who pummels his dad's punching bag instead of another boy's body is using his anger energy to get a good workout.

One girl admits, "I beat up my stuffed teddy bears whenever I'm angry, and I feel much better afterward. I never hurt anyone or break anything."

Sensei offers his ideas. "Unhealthy anger confuses and abuses. Don't sit around thinking, *I'll hurt him like he hurt me. . . . He deserves it. . . . I can't stand it anymore. . . . I feel like breaking something.* These thoughts will just stir up trouble. Don't pick fights. Pick friends to talk with about your bad feelings."

What can you do to control your anger?

Erin: *"Instead of sitting and sulking in a bad mood, find a friend. Do something fun."*

Deanna: *"Get rid of bad feelings by thinking about the things you are good at."*

Patricia: *"If you can't find anything good about yourself, ask a friend what they like about you."*

Ivan: *"Instead of looking for trouble, play a sport. Ride your bike. Get yourself tired out. Sleep it off. Leave your anger behind."*

Now it is time to consider some physical actions. Learning any new action requires careful and consistent practice. This is especially true of self-defense movements because a mistake can result in injury. Simply reading about the following techniques and advice is not enough; study them, talk about them, have your friends quiz one another, and consider signing up for a self-defense class!

POWER 3 . . . .
How to "Stand Up" and "Withstand" Trouble

If you can't get out of the way of an aggressive pusher, you can withstand the force with resistant postures. Strong stances prepare you to "withstand" a powerful push or pull, or "stand with" the strength of a mountain if you are confronted by an equal or slightly greater force. Learning to balance yourself against a tough bully is not the same as learning to stand on one leg! You will need to practice the basics of both sturdy and mobile postures.

To keep your balance, remember to:

1 BRACE YOURSELF

2 STAY ALERT

3 LOWER YOUR CENTER OF GRAVITY

4 BEND YOUR KNEES

5 WIDEN YOUR STANCE

KEEP YOUR BALANCE

BRACE YOURSELF A four-legged creature is much more stable than a two-legged human. So no matter how you stand, there is always a direction from which you can be pushed over. To remain stable against a forceful push, firmly place one leg behind you to offer resistance.

STAY ALERT

LOWER YOUR CENTER OF GRAVITY

STAY ALERT When you spot trouble coming, it's easier to prepare for action.

LOWER YOUR CENTER OF GRAVITY Your center of gravity is located about an inch below your navel. Place your navel lower than an opponent's to increase your balance.

BEND YOUR KNEES With straight, stiff legs you can be toppled like a statue. Keep your knees slightly bent and your legs relaxed for quick, evasive movements—as if you are standing on a small boat, ready to catch yourself if the boat rocks.

WIDEN YOUR STANCE When your feet are close together, you can be knocked off-balance easily from any direction. Place your feet at least shoulder width apart to stabilize your torso.

BEND YOUR KNEES

WIDEN YOUR STANCE

BRACE YOURSELF

Three Pillars of Strength

Here are three postures that, like the stone pillars of a building, can support you against forceful pushes and pulls.

1 THE MOUNTAIN STANCE

"Believe you are a mountain of rock. Feel the strength in your legs," Sensei tells them. Justin cannot resist Ivan's push. His legs buckle. He stumbles backward. When Sensei tells him to widen his legs and lower his body, Ivan cannot budge him.

Josh's mountain stance withstands the push of five boys. That's 324 pounds of push!

Several girls grab Patricia's arm and yank. Patricia glides forward into the mountain stance. She resists them like a stubborn donkey.

2 THE IRON LEG STANCE

"Imagine that one of your legs is solid iron," Sensei instructs. "Place your iron leg behind you, straight and strong. Let your iron heel dig into the ground. Bend your front knee over your big toe. Lean forward slightly."

Tommy withstands Justin's full-strength shove. No one will be able to push Tommy down from the front when he masters the iron leg stance.

3 THE FIGHTING STANCE

The boxer squares off in a guarded posture. His hands are poised to shield and strike. His chin is lowered. Legs are bent for quick movements. Feet are placed shoulder width for balance against the shock of a blow. He faces his challenger on an angle so his vital body targets become hard to hit.

"Look out behind you!" Sensei cries. The group spins around, crouching into their fighting stances. Their teacher shouts commands: "Turn right, turn left, turn around," he yells. One girl is startled and forgets what to do.

"It's okay," Sensei tells her. "Calm yourself and think about the movement."

The Tree Game

Some coastal trees hold so firmly to the ground that even hurricane winds do not uproot them. In martial arts, the term *rooting* describes the strength of a person's stance. Imagine your feet have roots growing into the earth to hold your body steady.

"When your partner pushes or pulls you," Sensei advises, "become an immovable tree. Root into a deep stance."

Daniel tugs Ivan off balance before he has a chance to put his roots down. Aja's legs strain against Erin's strong pull.

The class learns that with just three stances they can become solid fortresses against forceful pushes or pulls.

POWER 4 ·····················
Vital Targets, Pressure Points, and Body Weaknesses

"If you were threatened, what parts of your body would you defend first?"

"My nose?" Ivan answers.

Sensei shakes his head. "The nose hurts when struck but even with a broken or bloody nose you can still defend yourself. There are more important targets to consider."

WHAT ARE VITAL TARGETS?

Vital targets are areas of the body that, when struck, can be easily damaged and alter normal functioning. A blow to any vital target will cause pain or serious injury and will reduce your ability to defend yourself.

A strike to the eyes will cause temporary or permanent blindness. You cannot protect yourself if you cannot see.

A blow to the throat can cause serious injury or death. Your major nerves, air passageway, arteries, and neck vertebrae are all vulnerably exposed. A severe blow here can result in unconsciousness, suffocation, or paralysis.

The solar plexus is a nerve center deep in the body core. A direct blow can cause spasms and shock.

Males are most sensitive to **strikes between the legs**. Fritz remembers an accidental knee to his groin during a game of football. He felt a crippling pain.

"The same targets karate students use against their opponents are also points you do not want to have struck," Sensei explains. He shows them sixteen traditional martial art targets on the front of the body.

Q *I got punched in the ribs once and couldn't breathe. Are the ribs vital targets?*

A *People struck in the ribs or abdomen often get the wind knocked out of them because the diaphragm, the main muscle of breathing, spasms when hit forcefully. Blows to the knees or finger joints can also painfully twist or hyperextend them. If a body part that is struck disables you from protecting yourself further, it can be considered a vital target.*

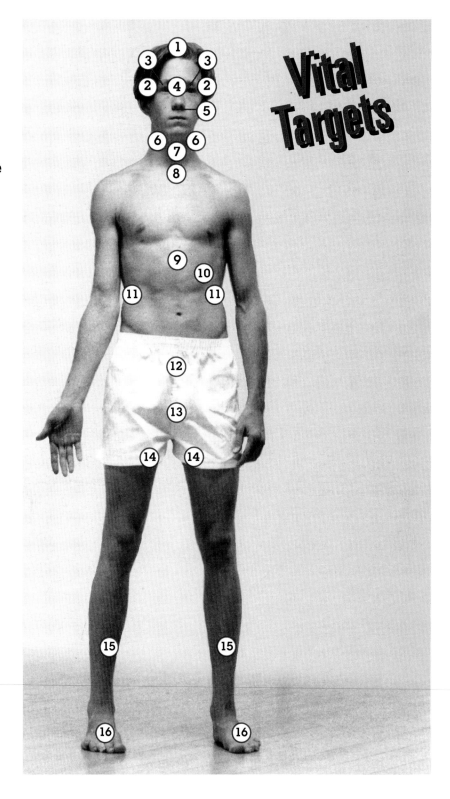

1. Skull
2. Temple
3. Eyes
4. Bridge of Nose
5. Philtrum
6. Neck
7. Adam's Apple
8. Windpipe
9. Solar Plexus
10. Sternal Angle
11. Floating Ribs
12. Abdomen
13. Groin
14. Thigh
15. Shin
16. Instep

Vital Targets

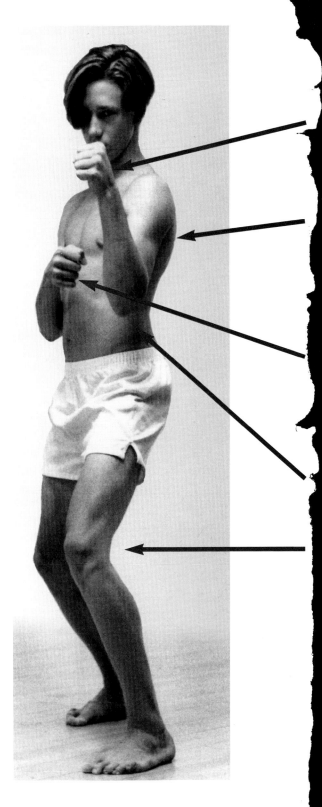

How to Protect Body Targets

TILT YOUR CHIN DOWNWARD
Tilting the head offers some eye
protection and covers your throat
so that a fist cannot fit under it.

**ANGLE AWAY FROM AN
ATTACKER** Never face someone
directly if you suspect trouble. Turn
sideways or slightly to one side to
protect your groin and solar plexus
and move immediately away.

**COVER YOUR SOLAR PLEXUS
WITH YOUR FIST** For further
protection, place your fist like
a sentry in front of, but not
touching, this spot.

DRAW YOUR ELBOWS INWARD
Tuck your elbows into your side to
protect the ribs.

BEND YOUR KNEES Placing
your knees over your toes
prevents your legs and ankles from
being damaged.

The fighting stance will safeguard
nearly all the significant targets on
the front of your body. In a serious
confrontation this stance, coupled
with the proper evasive and resistance
techniques, is an ideal strategy.

Ancient warriors noticed that strikes to nonvital areas of an enemy's body sometimes caused immediate pain, numbing, or paralysis. Traditional Chinese doctors also discovered hundreds of energy spots all over the body that could heal an illness when touched. The warriors' need to defend themselves in combat and the Chinese doctors' need to find cures for their ailing patients both led to the study of pressure points.

PRESSURE POINTS

Pressure points are generally found in areas of the body you would never consider vulnerable. Arm and leg points are easier to reach and activate than vital targets. Activating them can cause muscle and joint weakness. Hundreds of these points have been discovered. When they are pressed, struck, rubbed, tapped, slapped, or vibrated, singly or in combinations, mild numbing to immediate unconsciousness, or even death, can result. The study of self-defense pressure points is a complex martial art. However, there are several non-lethal points that are helpful in escaping from grabs or grips.

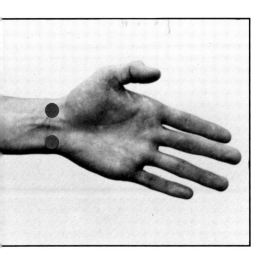

Wrist Points

There are two pressure points located on the wrist. Firm finger pressure applied to these spots can weaken the grip of anyone who has seized hold of you. Pressing these points does not cause pain. It simply stops the energy flow into the hand. You will experiment with these wrist points in Power 7 to escape from holds.

Sensitive Spots

Far less force or pressure is needed to create pain in weak or sensitive areas of the body. These areas should be considered only if you cannot free yourself from a larger, stronger assailant who intends to harm you.

Josh bends Sensei's pinky back with a finger lock. "That's enough!" he signals. Even a master feels pain when his fingers are bent.

Tommy demonstrates an ear twist and eyelid pinch on himself. "Ouch! That hurts just looking at it," Josh says.

A sharp palm strike under the nose will cause the eyes to water. If your hands are pinned, you can butt the nose with your forehead. The skin on the inner thighs is very sensitive to pinching and twisting. The pain can cause an attacker to release his grip. Raking your heel down the shinbone causes pain. The instep, or top of the foot, has many small bones. A heel stomp there can cause crippling pain.

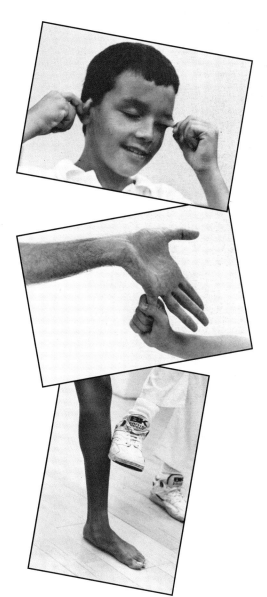

POWER **5** • • • • • • • • • • • • • • • • • • •
Many Ways to Defend

Smash! Clang! *Quick motions of the knight's sword and shield ward off the lethal rain of the battle-ax's blows. The hungry raccoon pounces on its victim. The turtle's head and legs retract into its impenetrable bunker. The spry little mongoose leaps aside, easily dodging the lightning lunges of the poisonous habu snake.*

Everywhere in nature living things demonstrate an impressive array of survival skills in the form of blocks, shields, and evasions. Humans have their own unique defenses. There are dozens of ways to guard against grabs, pushes, slaps, punches, or kicks by simply using your arms and legs. In fact, you have already used many natural self-defense techniques by dodging balls and insects, playing tag, or competing in sports and games of skill and action.

Don't Get Hit!

In self-defense your first goal is to avoid getting hit or grabbed. To accomplish this, it is often necessary to use one part of your body to protect another. Blocking or shielding uses an expendable body part (one less important) to protect a vital body part (one very important). Your arms and legs can take a lot of punishment, so they are considered expendable body parts. Just as medieval knights defended themselves from lethal blows, you can condition and position your limbs to shield or deflect strikes or attempted grabs. You don't need a lot of power to divert a strike if you correctly time your block to intercept the strike.

You don't need a lot of power to divert a strike.

Shields Up!

Shielding is the action of placing your arms or legs in the way of an incoming strike. The famous heavyweight boxing champion Muhammad Ali was pushed up against the ropes in one of his title bouts. His powerful opponent, George Foreman, pummeled Ali's head and body. The champ drew his arms to his torso. He tucked his head into his hands. He called his protective maneuver the "Rope-a-Dope." He absorbed blow after punishing blow. When Foreman's arms tired, Ali used the opportunity to defeat his opponent and win the championship. By covering his head and trunk, Ali spared his vital targets from injury. It was a good example of the protective powers of shielding.

...acticing self-defense means
...ing out the real movements
... typical conflicts without hurt-
... your partner. It's important
... follow these rules when
...u're perfecting techniques:

- Be considerate
- Use caution
- Say "Stop!" or tap your
  partner's body if you feel
  any pain
- Pay close attention to
  the details of all your
  techniques
- Begin your practice with
  half-strength blocks,
  strikes, or grips
- Use full-force holds only
  when you and your partner
  are both confident you can
  do the movement
  correctly and with the
  proper self-control
- Never trip or throw a partner who has not mastered
  break falls (the technique
  of falling without injury)
  and without a soft,
  unobstructed surface to
  land on. Always warn your
  partner first.

Low, Middle, High Block!

Another way to deal with attacks is to parry them. *Parry* is a French fencing term. It means to deflect or ward off. In martial arts, parrying movements are called *blocks*.

Three simple, single-forearm blocking motions can protect the entire front of your body from all kinds of attacking motions. A high block protects the face and the top of the head. A middle block protects the chest, solar plexus, and ribs. A low block defends against kicks and other low strikes.

After acquainting themselves with the basic blocking motions, the group drills them from different stances to learn the actual feel and proper timing for intercepting and redirecting strikes.

like a golf club . . .

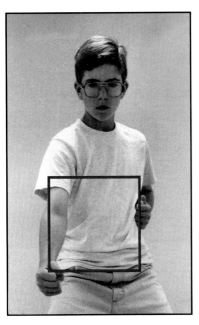

Robert swings his forearm downward like a golf club to defend against kicks and other low strikes.

like a windshield wiper . . .

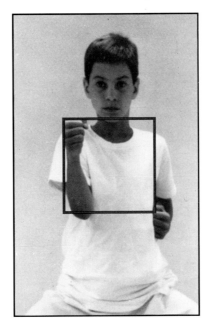

Ignacio sweeps his forearm across his torso like a windshield wiper. He protects his chest, solar plexus, and ribs.

like an umbrella

Aja sweeps her forearm upward like an umbrella, protecting her face and the top of her head.

Pretending he's a kidnapper, the teacher reaches out to grab Erin. She swats his hand away and bolts to freedom.

BLOCKS

The class agrees that you should get away from trouble as fast as you can. However, if you must protect yourself, there are many ways to use hands and arms defensively.

Shield with your arms

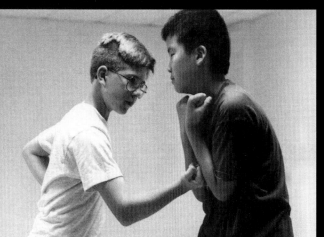

Block with the inside of your forearm

X-block to protect your head

Knife hand block

Use your hands to ward strikes away

Fold a grabbed arm and block

Block punches and kicks simultaneously

If all else fails,
curl up to protect vital targets

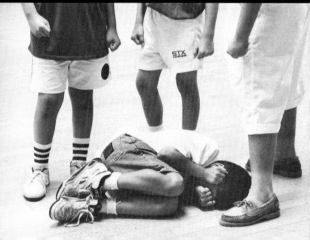

EVASIONS: GETTING OUT OF HARM'S WAY

If you're attacked, don't stand still. Move!

An evasion uses your legs and torso to get out of the way of a threatening move. Anyone who has played tag, dodgeball, or similar activities has practiced evading. Many young wild animals develop incredible dodging abilities by playing hunt and hide games. They learn to avoid the lethal fangs or claws of their predators.

If you're attacked, don't stand still. Move! A moving target is harder to hit than a stationary one. Sensei tells a story of how his younger brother got punched square in the face by an angry bully.

"If he had only moved, even a little, he would have been safe," the teacher reflects.

To evade a grab or push, take short, quick steps away by backpedaling or sidestepping. Jump, duck, dodge, or pivot like the matador who easily avoids the raging bull. Be careful not to fall down.

Q *Is one direction better to evade in than another?*

A *It depends upon the situation. Often the safest direction is toward the outside of an arm. If an opponent swings a left arm down upon your head, move to the right. This will make it difficult for him to hit you.*

POWER 6
Natural Weapons

Your body is equipped to both block (defend) and strike (offend). Many wild animals use their paws, claws, or powerful back leg muscles for protection. Likewise, your arms and legs can be trained to snap or thrust in every direction with speed and power. One self-defense master could throw eleven strikes in two seconds. Others demonstrate power by breaking or crushing wood, bricks, and tiles.

The Hands

Rolling the fingers into a tight flesh and bone ball protects them from injury. It also molds a penetrating hard-knuckle striking surface.

Asian martial arts masters often choose the open hand, in the form of chops, spears, palms, and ridgehands, over the closed fist. A master of the Chinese martial art tai chi chuan demonstrated the palm's power. He slapped a two-and-a-half-inch-thick slab of concrete. It split in half. *The palm has power!*

American actors have often portrayed frontiersmen as tough-fisted pioneers who carved legends into American history with their bare knuckles.

Open or closed hands, even the sides of your arm, make good striking tools. They can be launched quickly from any position.

To make a fist, roll your fingers tightly. Lock them in place with your thumb on the outside.

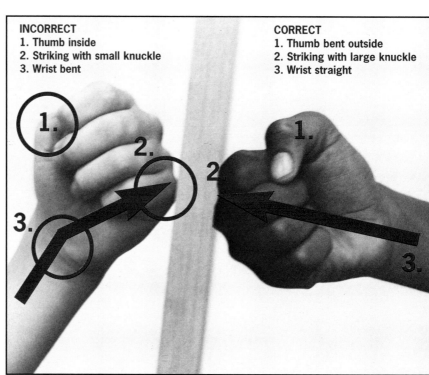

INCORRECT
1. Thumb inside
2. Striking with small knuckle
3. Wrist bent

CORRECT
1. Thumb bent outside
2. Striking with large knuckle
3. Wrist straight

One of Sensei's students tucks his thumb inside his fingers.

"Punching like that will hurt your hand," the teacher explains. "Your thumb becomes like a nut inside a nutcracker."

The group starts a striking drill. Punches snap at imaginary targets. Then everyone hits a leather pad to get the feel of contact.

Pop! Josh's two big knuckles sink into the soft red leather.

"Do your punches feel fast or slow, weak or strong?" the teacher asks. "Could you hit a dime-sized spot five times in a row?"

Ignacio has quick hand speed. He knows that a powerful strike is a fast one. Sensei times the speed of his punch from initiation to hit with an electronic pad. It registers one-third of a second! Robert steps up to the pad and sinks into a fighting stance. He puts his whole body into his punch.

Pow! His bigger size gives him a lot of power.

The teacher shows them four elbow strikes. Elbows are used to defend yourself when you are too close to punch.

HAND STRIKES

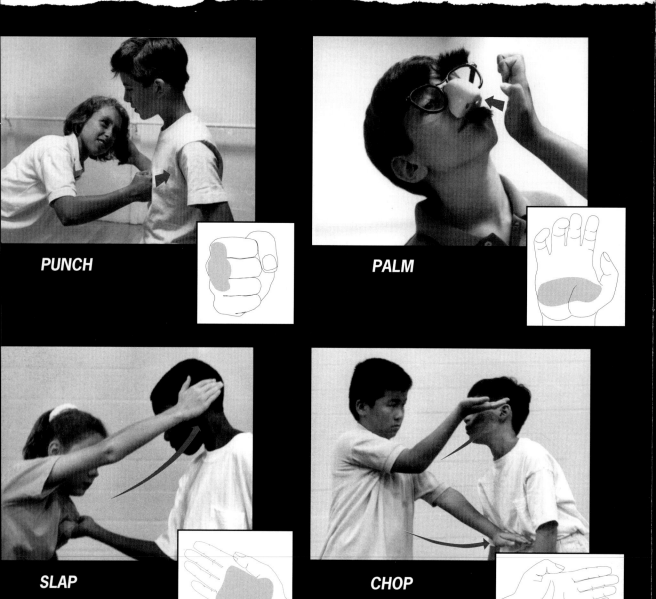

PUNCH

PALM

SLAP

CHOP

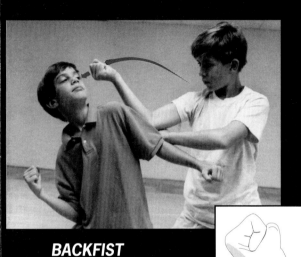

BACKFIST

Remember that a powerful blow to any part of the human body can cause pain and injury. Never strike someone unless you have exhausted all other means of resolving the conflict. Always attempt to distance yourself from the trouble first!

SPEAR

Instep

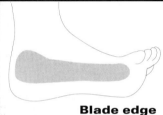

Blade edge

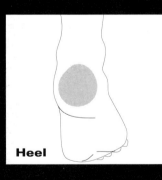

Heel

Ball of the foot

The Feet

Kicking is the hallmark of every exciting karate and kung fu movie. Heel thrusts, flying crescent kicks, jump-spinning back kicks, and wood-splintering blade-edge kicks terminate the toughest movie villains. Kicks unleash tremendous force. But most movie fight scenes with spectacular head-high sport strikes are not practical in a real conflict unless you are a trained expert. The most effective kicks are aimed low and delivered quickly.

"Phew! This is tiring," Ivan admits. He doesn't kick much. He feels that his legs are a little tight and slow.

"I love kicking," Josh tells him. He leaps into the air and kicks a pad six feet above! Josh is only four feet six inches tall. "I've been kicking for four years! You can do it, Ivan. Just stick with it."

FOOT STRIKES

heel stomp

side kick

back kick

knee strike

front kicks

side thrust

u get
ouble,
might
have
chance
eact.

Choose Your Weapon

The late, great kung fu master Bruce Lee studied long and hard to find the best, most effective methods of defending himself. You, too, will have to discover your best moves and strategies because if you get in trouble, you might only have one chance to react. Self-defense beginners who can't decide what to practice first should consider the following:

1 **Your legs are best used for balance or to kick low on an opponent. High kicks sacrifice equilibrium. If you fall or your leg is grabbed, you're likely to get into worse trouble.**

2 **Legs are stronger than the arms. They can deliver much greater power but require much more conditioning to be accurate.**

3 **Your arms are more coordinated than your legs. Hand strikes are faster to learn, more accurate, and the quickest means of protection.**

Trips and Flips

Kicks and punches are not your only means of protection. The martial art of judo teaches defensive throws and takedowns. Trips, flips, and sweeping movements can take an opponent off his feet. An assailant may think twice about harming you if you send him crashing to the ground.

"Ooh!" Robert twirls Josh like a human baton with a powerful hip throw. *Thump!* A little dazed and slow to get up, Josh is happy the floor is soft and that he has learned to fall safely.

Power 7 introduces some techniques for throwing an opponent off balance.

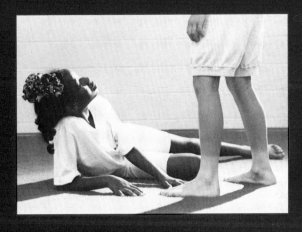

Down but not defeated, Aja's scissor action drops Patricia.

POWER **7** · · · · · · · · · ·
Great Escapes

Strong blocks or fast, powerful kicks and punches won't help you if someone immobilizes your arms and legs. If you're grabbed or wrestled to the ground, there are still many things you can do to defend yourself or free yourself from such holds.

Ignacio tells the group, "A bully once crunched my neck in a headlock. I couldn't breathe. The more I struggled to escape, the harder he squeezed. My head felt like it was in a vise. I was scared."

"Let's practice escaping from some common grips and locks," directs Sensei.

WRIST GRIPS

A tug-of-war begins as class members try to force their arms free from a wrist lock.

"You've fallen into a common trap," Sensei points out. "Whenever someone grabs you, they expect you will pull away. Naturally, they are ready to resist. In self-defense, we do the unexpected. Instead of struggling against the hold, follow this one simple rule:

To escape from any wrist grip, simply circle your hands around their wrists, either clockwise or counterclockwise. And if your circle doesn't work one way, then rotate it in the other direction."

The Japanese samurai warriors were skilled at escaping from their enemies' grips. These fierce fighters developed the art of jujitsu—a means of using leverage and their opponents' natural weaknesses to escape from a hold, loosen a grip, or disarm them. For every lock the enemy applied against them, the jujitsu expert discovered a key to escape from it.

WRIST GRIP 1—Left Hand Grabs a Right Wrist

"Twist your palm up, turn your wrist sideways, then lift your arm out of the grip." Sensei demonstrates for Josh. "Wedge the thin side of your arm between Robert's thumb and fingers." Josh obeys. His hand slips easily out of Robert's grasp.

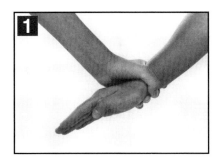

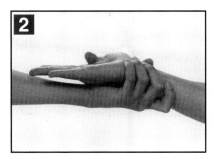

Twist palm up . . .

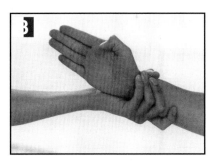

turn wrist sideways . . .

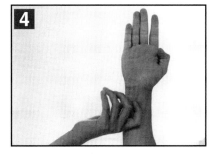

lift arm out

WRIST GRIP 2—Right Hand Grabs a Right Wrist

Justin imagines his arm is the second hand of a clock. He follows the teacher's explanation. Six o'clock to twelve, over the top and back to six.

"Wow! That's easy to slip out of!" he exclaims.

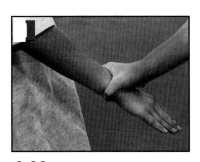

6:00 . . .

to 12:00, over the top . . .

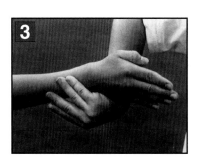

back to 6:00

STRANGLE

Dan grabs Josh in a strangle. To escape from this dangerous choke hold requires careful practice. Josh twists to the side he's grabbed on. He first restores oxygen to his throat by pulling Dan's elbow down and placing his chin in the bend of Dan's elbow. He can breathe now. To escape, Josh puts his foot behind Dan's front leg. He bends and twists. Dan loses balance and hurtles toward the ground.

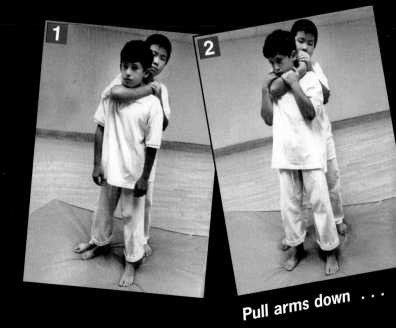

Pull arms down . . .

REAR CHOKE

"Gulp!" Josh barely has a chance to swallow when Ignacio sneaks up behind and chokes him. All of a sudden Josh disappears under his arms.

"Hey, how did you do that?" Ignacio asks with a puzzled look on his face.

"Simple," Josh says. "I slipped my leg behind yours and twisted under your hands."

Erin walks over and asks Ignacio to grab her. In a flash she finds his little pinkies and pries his hands open.

"There's more than one way to get out of this hold," she says.

put chin in elbow . . .

foot behind front leg · · · bend and twist

Bend knees, step back . . .

twist around and under hands · · ·

escape

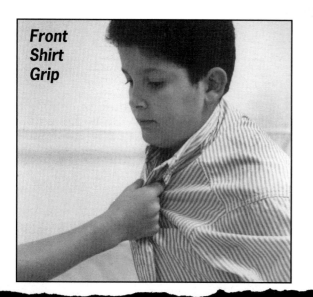

Front Shirt Grip

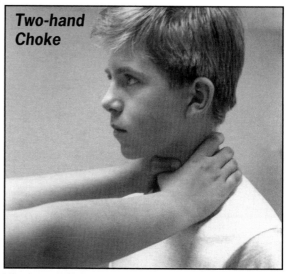

Two-hand Choke

A MULTIPURPOSE ESCAPE MOVEMENT

Sensei demonstrates a multipurpose escape movement that can be used effectively against a front shirt grip, and a one- or two-arm push or choke. After a few minutes of practicing, Justin calls out to the teacher.

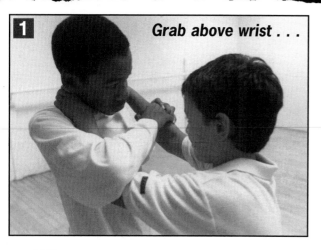

1 *Grab above wrist . . .*

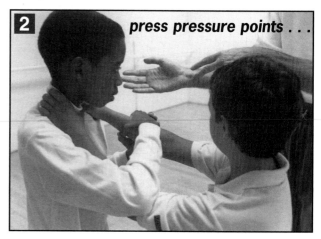

2 *press pressure points . . .*

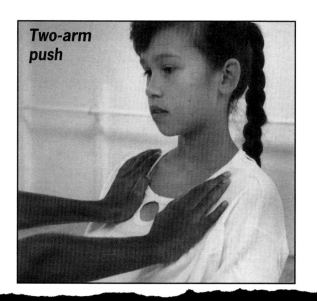

Two-arm push

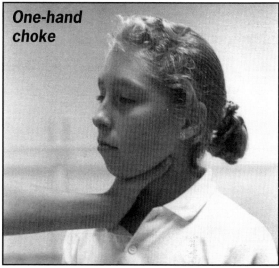

One-hand choke

"Sensei, this technique doesn't work," he says, frustrated that he cannot budge his partner, Tommy. "He's even smaller than me!"

"You have to activate the pressure points on the wrists, Justin. Grab just above Tommy's wrist joint. Press the two points. When you're grabbed with a right arm, twist it to your right." Justin readjusts his grip. He clenches Tommy's wrist and rotates his arm. The grip is broken!

3 twist arm . . .

4 escape grip

REAR BEAR HUG

Deanna grabs Patricia from behind. "How about a hug?" she asks.

Patricia ponders her escape plan. Poke her fingers into Deanna's groin? Stomp her instep? Rake her shin with her foot? Grab a piece of skin on the inside of her thigh and twist? Patricia finally decides to step behind Deanna's leg and squat down.

"Thanks for the hug, but I've got to go!" Patricia says. Sensei cautions Patricia that if Deanna hadn't been startled enough to let go as she fell to the floor, Patricia might have gone down with her. He adds, "If you are lifted off your feet in the bear hug, you may need to strike to the eyes, nose, or groin to escape."

Plan escape . . .

FULL NELSON

Tommy feels pressure on his neck and back. Ignacio is bending him in half.

"I give up," Tommy pleads. "He's too strong for me, Sensei." The teacher whispers into Tommy's ear.

"Try again," Tommy says with a grin. When Ignacio tries to bend him this time, Tommy places his hands on his own forehead. Ignacio's face reddens with strain. He cannot budge his victim. Suddenly, Tommy releases his hands, bends forward, and slips his foot behind Ignacio's leg. Ignacio is swept off balance.

"What do I do with him now?" Tommy asks, holding Ignacio like a large tote bag.

"Throw him, don't carry him," instructs Sensei. Tommy gets the idea. Ignacio gets dumped.

Lock fingers on forehead . . .

step behind leg . . .

thrust hips back . . .

squat and escape

release quickly and bend forward . . .

step behind legs . . .

lift opponent off balance . . .

throw and escape

CHICKEN WING
The Silver Dollar Escape

Robert cranks Deanna's arm behind her back. Deanna lifts up on her toes to escape the pressure.

"That makes it worse," the teacher explains. He places a silver dollar by her right foot. "It's yours, Deanna, if you can pick it up with your left arm." She bends to reach for the coin. Before she even realizes it, she escapes from the dreaded chicken wing.

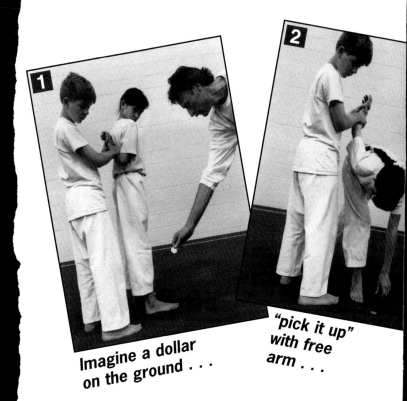

Imagine a dollar on the ground . . .

"pick it up" with free arm . . .

THE VISE GRIP HEADLOCK

Tommy tightens his grip around Josh's neck. Josh slides his hand under Tommy's nose. He presses in and pushes up as if trying to stop Tommy from sneezing. *Gesundheit!* Josh frees his neck from the headlock. Tommy rubs his sore nose.

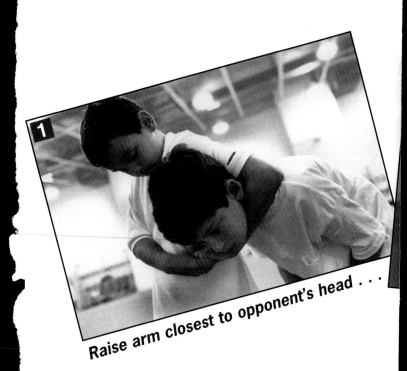

Raise arm closest to opponent's head . . .

move around . . .

and behind opponent . . .

escape grip

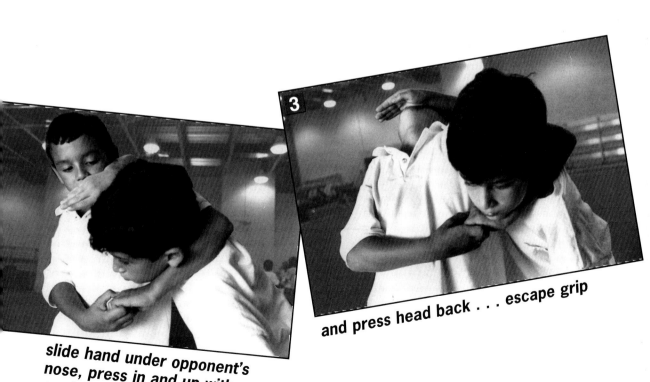

slide hand under opponent's nose, press in and up with a sawing motion . . .

and press head back . . . escape grip

Lift arms up · · ·

swing arms out at sides . . .

lift knee, push into opponent · · ·

thrust hips up and roll to side

DISMOUNT!

"What are you going to do now, tough guy?" Ivan jokes with Dan. "You'll never escape." He sits on Dan's stomach and pins his arms to the ground. Ivan is bigger and heavier. Dan struggles to push upward. Ivan forces him back down. Suddenly, Dan swings his arms to his sides. He lifts and pushes his knee into Ivan. With a quick thrust and twist of Dan's hips, Ivan goes flying.

"That's what I'm going to do," Dan says with an air of confidence.

There are hundreds of escape moves and several ways to get out of any single grip. If you can repeatedly escape from strong holds placed upon you by different people, then you know they work! Surprise is an important element of success. If an opponent knows what you are going to do, it will become difficult, even impossible, to escape unless you are an expert. You may need to strike to weaken a hold before you try your escape maneuver. Once you are out of the grip, run, get help, or fight back, if necessary.

"To learn additional escapes, find a book on jujitsu or enroll in a martial arts school," Sensei advises.

Part 3

Victorious generals devise great plans to win their wars. They call their plans *strategies*. Strategies are methods used to gain an objective or reach a goal. Sports teams plan strategies to use against opposing players to score first or the most. Strategies are decided before a contest or a conflict begins. Consider your safety now. Don't wait until trouble finds you. Do some preplanning. Forewarned is forearmed!

■Set Goals

To create a good plan, you need to set goals of what you want to accomplish. In self-defense the overall goals are to:

▶ **Find a peaceful, nonviolent solution to your problems whenever you can.**

▶ **Avoid troublesome ideas, persons, and places.**

▶ **Do whatever is reasonable to avoid injury or pain.**

Here are some special strategies for dealing with dangerous or hurtful situations.

Fitness
is one of
your most
natural
self-defense
powers.

■ Stay Fit

Exercise! A fit body is better prepared for the unexpected. Exercise is a great way to stay strong, healthy, and alert. Find a sport or physical activity to keep you limber and increase your strength and stamina. Fitness is one of your most natural self-defense powers.

■ Act Like a Victor, Not a Victim

On the African savannah, a hungry lion instinctively knows it would be dangerous to attack a healthy wildebeest. Likewise, bullies and assailants also seem to know who is the weakest and easiest person to pounce upon. To avoid being trouble's target, act like a victor, not a victim.

▶ **Stand tall. Don't hunch. Stick out your chest a little. Hold your head high.**

▶ **Stay alert. Use your eyes like lighthouse beacons roaming the sea for rough weather.**

▶ **Don't shuffle when you walk. Take confident steps.**

▶ **Make just enough eye contact to get a feeling about someone. Don't stare or glare back defiantly. This can be read as a challenge and lead to greater danger.**

▶ **If you find yourself in trouble, don't pretend that nothing is happening to you. Don't look down or roll your eyes. Take action.**

▶ **Speak clearly. Be assertive about your safety.**

▶ **Act quickly.**

■ To Speak or Not to Speak

Some mouths get people into trouble; others talk them out of it. Only you will know when to talk and what to say. Express yourself clearly! Let others know your feelings. Tell troublemakers that you want to find a peaceful solution to the problem. Quick thinking with the right words can prevent injury or pain.

Talking your way out of a problem might also be the absolutely wrong thing to do. Your danger may be so sudden that there is no time to speak. You will then have to resort to other actions.

■ If You Must Fight Back

All fighting is ugly and painful. Do not wait until you are in the midst of a problem to decide whether you could hurt someone who assaults you. Your confusion could mean the difference between life and death. Choose now what you would be willing to do to save yourself from injury or pain.

"I could never poke someone in the eyes," Aja says.

"I could," Ignacio confesses, "especially if someone tried to really hurt my younger brother."

Express yourself clearly!

Choose now what you would be willing to do to save yourself from injury or pain.

■When You Are Home Alone

There are many ways to keep yourself protected from intruders. You can take charge of your safety or reduce the fear of being alone if no one else will.

● If your parents are going out and you are afraid of staying at home, ask them to get you a baby-sitter. If they refuse, make arrangements to stay with a friend, relative, or neighbor until they return.

● If you must remain in the house, then have your parents or care-takers leave you two phone numbers, one where they can be reached and one of a nearby neighbor or relative who will be home while they are gone.

● Find out if your parents expect any people to stop by your house and what times they are expected.

● As soon as they leave, lock all entry doors, windows, and screens. Pull the curtains or lower the blinds in the room you are in, particularly if you are on the ground floor. This way no one can see you or tell that you're alone.

● At night, keep lights on in the main rooms and have a flashlight nearby with fresh batteries. Keep emergency numbers like the 911 emergency system or the police, fire, and first aid department numbers next to the phone.

● If you answer the phone, never say you are alone. Tell callers your parents cannot come to the phone. Ask them to leave their names and numbers.

● Don't watch scary shows. They can make you paranoid.

● Keep the volume of your TV, stereo, or CD player low enough to hear the phone, doorbell, and other house sounds.

● Do not answer the door for any stranger. If someone attempts to break in, call the police immediately. They will instruct you what to do next.

■ When Out Alone or in Unfamiliar Places

It has never been wise to wander or travel alone, especially in unfamiliar places and at night.

● When you're ready to go out, let at least one parent or a trustworthy adult know exactly where you are going and what time you plan to return. Whenever possible, give them a phone number where you can be contacted.

● Carry important phone numbers with you, along with enough change to make at least two emergency calls. Plan the safest route to your destination.

● While outside, walk with a friend if possible.

● Travel in well-lit, peopled areas.

● Be alert, vigilant, and curious at all times. Notice landmarks and observe where adults are congregating in case you need a fast getaway or need to summon help.

● Stay clear of corners, doorways, alleys, shrubs, parked vehicles where a person could hide and lunge out at you, and any other place that gives you the creeps.

● Steer clear of gangs and suspicious people. If followed, go immediately to a policeman, security officer, postal worker, or into a shop with customers.

● Always avoid deserted areas. Whenever you sense trouble, trust your feelings. Leave the area immediately.

● When you are inside a building, know where you are going. If you're unsure, ask a security guard, doorman, or building employee. It's a good idea upon entering a large building to inform security that you are there alone or have been separated from your parents.

● Stay clear of corner and back stairwells. Be wary of deserted corridors. Always walk down the center of an empty corridor.

● Before getting into an elevator, check to see who's inside. Once inside, stand near the control panel. Locate the emergency call button.

● If you have to use a public rest room, ask a friend, relative, or responsible adult either to wait for you to come out or accompany you inside.

Avoid the Stranger Danger

Don't trust strangers. If you are approached by one, keep a safe distance or run away. One rule is to stand at least a stranger's leg length away so you cannot be grabbed or struck.

If you see a suspicious person around your school or neighborhood, immediately inform your parents or teachers. Have them call the police.

You cannot always tell what a suspicious person looks like. Robbers, drug dealers, child abductors, and molesters can look like ordinary people. Trust your feelings. If someone makes you feel uneasy, keep away. Remember the height, weight, sex, the way that person looks and dresses, unusual marks on the body like scars, beards, and any odd characteristics. This information can help the police to locate the person quickly and keep you safe.

Draw Attention to Yourself

Anyone within earshot or eyesight can and should be summoned for help if you are in danger. Sound is a survival tool! Use your voice to draw attention to yourself.

▶ Yell, *"Fire! Help me! I am in trouble."* People often take notice when you yell "fire" to make sure nothing of theirs is burning.

▶ Don't just scream. Screaming does not convey any message that you are in trouble. However, a piercing scream in an assailant's ear can startle and injure the eardrum. It may give you time to escape.

▶ Learn to project your voice. Don't be embarrassed!

Remember: "A leg's length away keeps trouble at bay!"

Sound is a survival tool!

■ Use Hidden Tools

The bully pressed his face up to the frightened boy. The boy was so nervous he crumbled the chocolate chip cookie in his hand. Then he had an idea. He blew the crumbs in the bully's eyes and ran away.

Common objects on your person or in your immediate vicinity can protect you. To the untrained, these objects are hidden because they don't appear as protective aids. But a simple object can add extra reach or force to a block or a strike, or shield your body from a blow.

Do not carry knives or guns. These are extremely dangerous weapons, and they can easily be turned against you.

Look around. How many things on your person or in the immediate environment could you convert into a protective tool?

eyeglasses	**books**
combs	**magazines**
keys	**newspapers**
coins	**book bags**
jackets	**lunch boxes**
sweaters	**sticks**
belts	**umbrellas**
pens	**dirt**
pencils	**stones**

> A simple object can add extra reach or force to a block or a strike, or shield your body from a blow.

■If Someone Wants to Rob You

Your life is more valuable than anything you own. But your possessions may be more valuable than your life to a robber. Horrible tales of people murdered for two dollars are real tragedies. **If someone threatens to hurt or kill you for your money, hat, sunglasses, radio, jewelry, jacket, a ball, bike, or anything else they desire,** *give it to them!*

Never go with a stranger or a robber to any other location. The best precaution is not to carry anything of real value on your person when you are outside.

■Defend against an Aggressive Dog

Nearly a million people a year are attacked or bitten by aggressive dogs. If you are approached by a vicious neighborhood or stray dog, you have a good chance of avoiding being attacked or bitten if you do the following: **Stand still. Do not look the dog directly in the eyes. Look just over the top of its head. Do not shout or scream to scare it off. Speak softly. Then slowly back away while facing the dog. Don't run.** If the dog attempts to bite, use your arms and closed fists to protect vital body parts like the windpipe. If the dog continues to bite, roll into a ball on the ground. (See the picture on page 37.) Tuck your knees and head into your chest with your arms protecting your face.

Your life is more valuable than anything you own.

■Surviving a Bully

Below is a five-step plan for keeping your cool and staying in control when confronted by one or more aggressive individuals. Try each step. If the first doesn't work, move on to the next.

1 IGNORE
Don't listen to or believe any negative comments a bully makes about you. A bully cannot make you think you are weak, scared, worthless, ugly, or cowardly if you believe in yourself instead. Nobody's perfect. You do not have to be the subject of someone's jokes, jeering, mockery, intimidation, or physical abuse. Accept who you are.

2 SPEAK YOUR MIND WITH BOTH EYES OPEN
Bullies pick on people they don't think will stand up for themselves. It makes them feel powerful. Tell a bully you do not like what he or she is saying or doing to you. Look straight into the bully's eyes and say, *"No"* to any actions you dislike. A confident, strong verbal reaction can stop most bullies in their tracks. Keep your eyes on a bully so she or he doesn't pull any tricks. Be aware of your surroundings for a way to escape or get help. Don't turn your back until you are at a safe distance. Tell the bully you would be willing to find a peaceful solution to the problem. Tell him or her you would be willing to have a third person help you resolve the problem.

3 HANDS OFF!
Do not let a bully touch or push you. If a bully tries to push you, duck, dodge, pivot, move to the side, or use your powerful stances to become immovable. Say, "No!" or "Stop!" You don't have to strike someone for touching you, but try to react before you are touched. Most importantly, keep your balance, and stay calm and relaxed.

4 DEFEND If a bully tries to physically hurt you, defend with blocks, shields, and evasions. Don't crumble into a heap on the floor. Stand up for yourself. Keep your balance.

5 FIGHT INTELLIGENTLY AND RESPONSIBLY
Strike someone only as a last resort to protect yourself from immediate or continued pain or injury. Fighting smart is about not getting injured. Consider your safety first!

Do not keep your attack a secret. There are many people who will want to help you, but you must tell them what happened.

There is no reason, no matter how strict your parents are, that they should cause physical injury to you.

■ If Assaulted by an Adult

It is against the law for an adult to strike or harm a minor. A minor is any person seventeen years or younger. It is rare that a young person can defeat an adult. If an adult tries to hurt, abuse, or abduct you, act quickly. Use your escape techniques. Draw attention to yourself. Yell, "Fire!" Make noise. Knock things over. Place obstacles between you and your assailant. Throw things. Use your self-defense skills. If you are grabbed, bite and scratch. Pinch and pull hair, and if in serious danger strike the eyes with fingers spread. Get away to a safe place and get help immediately!

■ Against Family Abuse

All parents have different ideas about raising their children. Some are stricter than others. However, there is no reason, no matter how strict your parents are, that they should cause physical injury to you. If you believe you are being unduly or unfairly hurt by a parent, brother or sister, relative, or friend of the family, contact an adult you feel safe and comfortable talking with. Tell that person what is happening and ask him or her to get you help. If you do not know of anyone to speak with, contact a police officer, teacher, school counselor, doctor, hospital emergency worker, or religious official. Ask them if they will keep the information confidential from those who have abused you. You have equal rights to be respected and protected from bodily harm regardless of your age, race, or sex.

■ "PURR"

When a cat is happy and peaceful, it purrs. The letters PURR will help you to remember the four qualities vital to a happy, peaceful, nonviolent, and safe life. They are:

PEACE **Always look for peaceful solutions to your problems.**

UNDERSTANDING **We are all different. We think differently. Try to understand differences rather than forcing your attitudes or ideas upon others. Choose sharing. It's better to walk away from a problem saying, "I understand that person," rather than saying, "I am right. He is wrong." Understanding differences reduces the chances of a conflict getting worse.**

RIGHT ATTITUDE **Act with a healthy, positive attitude. Do not try to teach an opponent "a lesson he deserves." Instead, try to lessen any bad feelings or injurious actions.**

RIGHT TECHNIQUE **Choose the right technique for the right moment. The right technique might be a simple peacemaking comment: "Let's be friends instead of fighting." It might have to be a strong stance, a simple block, a punch, or a kick. Whatever it is, execute your movement with what the Japanese call *kime* (focus). With *kime* all your powers are used to bring a speedy and, if possible, peaceful solution to your problems.**

Part 4

WHAT IF IT HAPPENED TO YOU?

Let's see how well you could protect yourself with the new powers you have gained. Eleven pictures are presented here that depict a variety of aggressive or violent conflicts. Imagine that you are the victim in each scene. How would you feel? How would you react? How could you solve the conflict with the least amount of upset, injury, or pain? Look carefully at each scene. Discuss the scenes with others. To

QUESTION
Look at each picture and ask yourself what you might do . . .

make it more challenging, ask your friends or classmates to role-play the aggressor(s). Slowly talk and act out some healthy solutions.

There is more than one correct response for each situation. After you have decided what you would do, turn the page. Some intelligent actions are suggested. But remember—in any situation, the most appropriate action depends upon the individual behavior of the people involved and can only be determined by *you*.

ANSWER
After looking at each picture, turn the page and you will find some intelligent solutions.

Q.▶

THE PROBLEM This angry stranger is losing his temper. He may hurt or further embarrass you. He is not being reasonable. He unfairly wants your seat.

"Get out of my seat!"

An angry boy is shouting.

◀A. ▪ 1 "Get out of my seat!"

SELF-DEFENSE ACTIONS Be polite. Do not get angry. Keep your hands in your lap to ward off any aggressive physical actions. He does not have the right to pull you out of your seat. If you begin to feel upset, breathe deeply to keep yourself calm. Use the exercises on pages 20 and 21 to reduce fear or anger. Do not provoke the boy by yelling, screaming, or refusing to answer. Do not act willing to fight over the seat. There are plenty of empty seats around. You could be just as comfortable sitting somewhere else. Look around for support. An usher or adult may mediate your dispute over the seat. Attempt to calm the angry person by talking in a soft, slow manner. Acknowledge his anger. You could say:

"You look angry. I'd be happy to give you my chair."

"I would like to sit in this seat, but I will move."

"Perhaps you have mistaken me for someone else. Is everything all right? You look very angry. I hope you are not angry with me. I don't want to make you angry! Of course, you can have this seat."

If you feel unjustly confronted after giving up your seat, tell the usher or management that you have been approached by an angry person who unfairly demanded that you get out of your seat.

THE PROBLEM You are being unjustly teased and ganged up on. You are being emotionally abused. Abuse hurts no matter what form it takes.

"Crybaby!"

They have been teasing you all week.

A. ■ 2 "Crybaby!"

SELF-DEFENSE ACTIONS Be assertive. Tell the girls you do not like being teased and called a crybaby. These are hurtful remarks. Your words may not stop them from saying what they want, but you have the right to express your dislike of their actions. You do not have to stand there and take their abusive teasing. And you should not let them put their hands on you.

If possible, keep a distance from these people or find a different route home. If they are your friends, consider finding others who will accept you for who you are. Don't hang around with people who do not make you feel good about yourself.

Q. ▶

THE PROBLEM Your feelings are warning you that something is not right.

"Is he following me?"

You feel uneasy, but you don't want to miss your favorite T.V. show.

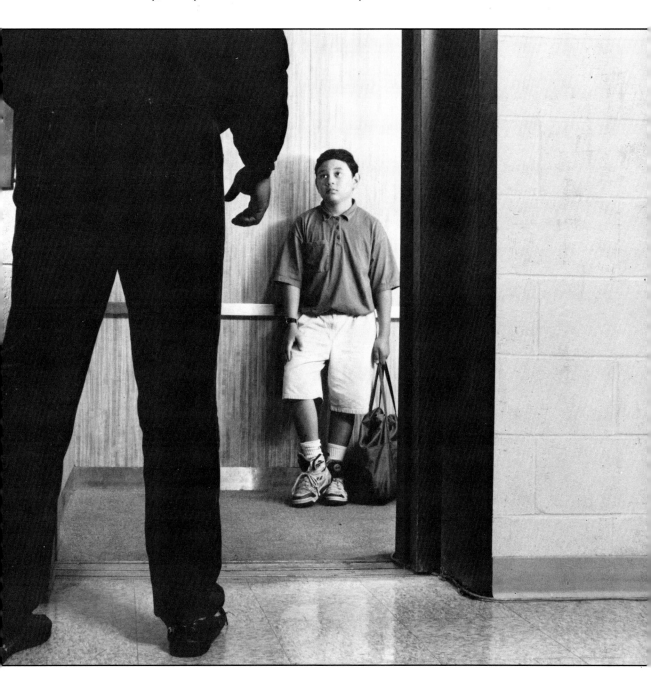

3 *"Is he following me?"*

SELF-DEFENSE ACTIONS Trust your feelings! Forget about seeing your TV show. Your safety comes first. Get off the elevator! Act confident and remain calm.

Whenever you step into an elevator, stand near the control panel. If the door is open and you are aggressively approached, press the emergency button. This will keep the door open. Get out of the elevator any way you can. Once out, get the attention of any responsible adult in the hallway. Tell the person that you do not want to go up on the elevator with the stranger inside because he frightens you, and ask for an escort to your floor. Immediately notify your parents or the landlord that you felt afraid of a strange man in the elevator.

Give a description of the stranger to your parents. This information will make it easier to identify him if he reappears.

THE PROBLEM You are being held without your consent and physically abused. You are suffering pain and possible injury from the towel.

"Hold him!"

The towel stings your arm. The bully readies to snap it again.

4 **"Hold him!"**

SELF-DEFENSE ACTIONS Tell the bully to stop. Tell him you are being hurt, and you don't like it. If he doesn't stop, immediately use the escape described on page 50 to get out of the stranglehold. Use the pressure points on page 31 if you need to weaken the grip.

If the person is too strong, you can rake your heel along his shin, heel stomp to the small bones of his foot, or pinch and twist the skin on the inside of his thigh. Then try the escape technique again.

Yell, "Fire! Help!" to draw attention to yourself.

Once free, grab the gym bag on the floor and shield yourself against the towel snaps.

If you break free, run to where there are people. Report the incident immediately to the nearest employee or staff person.

THE PROBLEM Your feelings are out of control. You are having negative and destructive thoughts.

5

"Hey, watch it!"

He accidentally spills your food. You don't have any money to buy another drink. You want to knock him down.

 **A.** ■ **5** *"Hey, watch it!"*

SELF-DEFENSE ACTIONS Accidents happen! It's natural to be upset in this case, but wishing to harm the other person is immature and unreasonable. Slowly count to ten. Take a deep breath with each count. Say to yourself, It's okay that I feel angry. It's okay that I feel upset. I was thirsty. I do not have any more money to buy another drink. But it's not right to hurt someone just because I am upset.

Express your anger. Tell the other boy that knocking your drink over made you really angry.

If you explain the incident to the boy who bumped you or to the person at the concession stand, he might replace whatever was spilled.

THE PROBLEM Your friend is out of control. He has lost his temper and is letting out his anger destructively. He is a danger to himself and others around him. One of your friends is hurt, and now he is going to hit you with the stick.

"He's hitting everyone!"

Your friend is out of control. He's coming after you.

A. ■ 6 "He's hitting everyone!"

SELF-DEFENSE ACTIONS Evade. Duck and dodge. Shout his name. Yell, "Mark, stop!" to get his attention. Use your arms to shield or block your face. Use any objects around you to shield yourself from being hit. Place yourself behind a tree, bush, bike, or car. Tell the other boy to get help. The three of you acting together could probably stop him or at least get the stick away. Try to calm the boy down. Tell him you are his friend, that you can see he is angry, and that you do not want to hurt or upset him further. Tell him to breathe deeply. It will make him feel better. Tell him it's okay to be angry but not to be hitting everyone. Ask him if he can explain why he is so angry. Run to a parent or neighbor. Get an adult to calm him down.

Q.▶

THE PROBLEM You're going to be physically hurt and possibly injured by a much stronger adult. This is not an act of discipline. This is an act of cruelty. This is child abuse.

"I've had enough!"

An adult is about to hit you.

A. 7 "I've had enough!"

SELF-DEFENSE ACTIONS Try to stay calm. Control your feelings. Accept responsibility if you have done something wrong. Speak out that you do not want to be hurt. Apologize. Say, "Please don't hurt me!" Attempt to calm the other person down. Call out her name. Ask her to stop. Call in a responsible adult or family member, whose presence or intervention might stop you from being hit further.

Shield your vulnerable targets with your arms if you are hit repeatedly. The arms can take much more abuse than your head, face, or torso.

Yell "Fire! Help me!" if the beating continues to the point of injury or if you think it may stop the attack.

THE PROBLEM You are being pressured to do something both illegal and distasteful to you. The group's action is called negative peer pressure. Peer pressure is common in young adult groups, when everybody is forced to bond together with like thoughts and ideas. Some peer pressure may be healthy and supportive. This example is negative and destructive.

"Are you with us, or are you a chicken?" Your friends want you to help them steal something.

A. 8 "Are you with us?"

SELF-DEFENSE ACTIONS Express yourself. Tell your friends that their thinking is wrong and destructive. Suggest more positive things to do, like going to the movies, playing a video game, or playing a sport.

If they still insist that you join them, simply say no! Tell them you do not want to be part of their activities. If they won't listen, then make an excuse to leave. If they continue to pressure you, wait until you are in an open area, assert again that you do not want to go with them, and walk away.

If they taunt, tease, or force you to join them, consider breaking off your friendship. You will not be happy doing things to which you are opposed.

THE PROBLEM You are being attacked and unjustly accused of stealing a boy's mitt. Your own anger is sending you out of control as well.

"It's a fight!"

Your teammate thinks you stole his mitt. He's not listening to reason.
He punches you in the face. You're startled.

 **9 "It's a fight!"**

SELF-DEFENSE ACTIONS Immediately use your arms to block or shield his punches. At the same time, lower your center of gravity into a strong stance to regain your balance. Use the front shirt grip escape on page 52.

Put your own ego aside, and try to avoid making the fight worse. Take his first punch and drop to the ground. Tell him he wins. Remember, violence only leads to more violence. Safety is your main concern.

If none of the above actions can protect you from further blows, you may have to consider striking.

If he walks away with your mitt, let him go! There is no sense in placing yourself in jeopardy again. Tell your coach and your parents you were assaulted by a teammate and that your mitt was taken. Have them contact the aggressive boy's parents. Explain what happened. When you see the boy again, have an adult with you when you confront him. There's a good chance you can clear up the misunderstanding after you and he have calmed down. Accept that the incident was a misunderstanding. Forgive and forget, and you'll walk away feeling much better.

THE PROBLEM You are being taken somewhere without your permission. You are being improperly touched. You may be sexually abused, beaten, or abducted.

"Let me touch you!"

The adult takes you into a back room. He squeezes your arm tightly. He tells you his little game is just between you and him. He wants you to keep it a secret.

 **10 "Let me touch you!"**

SELF-DEFENSE ACTIONS Trust your feelings. This action is not right. Do not be passive. You must act. Nobody has the right to touch you without your permission, even if the other person says it's only a game. Tell the man to let go. If he does not let go, use a wrist escape and run to safety. Yell. Draw attention to yourself. Strike back. Bite, pinch, or scratch, if necessary. Whatever happens, tell someone. They will understand and protect you. Do not keep this incident a secret.

THE PROBLEM You are being bullied and physically abused. You are scared.

"You're not so tough!"

Ted's Story

11

▸A. ■ 11 *"You're not so tough!"*

SELF-DEFENSE ACTIONS The best action would be to stay clear of these boys altogether. Walking right past them is only asking for trouble. Ignore any of their hurtful comments. Tell the aggressive boys that you do not want to fight, and you do not want to get hurt. When the one boy steps out to push you, immediately run. If you cannot run, evade or drop into a strong stance. Use your blocks, shields, and evasions. Stay calm. Draw attention to yourself. Don't let them surround you. Stay on the outside of their circle.

If you are knocked to the ground, roll into a ball or use your arms and legs to shield or block any strikes. Use your kicks and punches as a last resort to prevent being injured. Look for common objects to add extra protection. When you have a chance, get up and leave the area. Lock yourself in a car.

Tell the principal, your friends, your teachers, and your family what happened. Give them a description of the boys. The more people you have on your side, the safer you will feel.

A safe kid is a happy one!

CHOOSE A HAPPY ENDING

No one is invincible. Anyone can be hurt, even with the best ideas and techniques in mind. But it's better to have some choices of action rather than none. A new power has been passed on to you. Don't be afraid to apply this knowledge if you are ever in trouble. A tool is worthless if you don't use it. If you want to build a safe, happy, and healing place, begin now to make smart choices and to take healthy actions. A safe kid is a happy one! If you practice peace and safety today, you choose a happy ending for tomorrow.